Scuttle's Big Wish

This book
belongs to

Scuttle's Big Wish

Sean & Ryan Delonas

SCHOLASTIC INC.
New York Toronto London Auckland Sydney
Mexico City New Delhi Hong Kong Buenos Aires

Scuttle loved cheese.
He liked other things, too—his little mouse hole,
his cozy straw bed, and, of course, his best friend, Tweet.
But cheese is what he loved most.

Getting cheese
was not easy.

There were mousetraps
and other dangers all
along the way.

Worst of all, there was
Pounce the Cat

Luckily,
Scuttle was really fast

and always managed
to scurry home safely.

One day, Scuttle
heard a faint cry.

"Help! Help!"

He peeped outside.

A golden beetle
was trapped
in a spider's web.

So Scuttle scampered
up the sticky web and
freed the beetle.

"Thank you,"
said the golden beetle.
"I am in your debt.
I will grant you any wish."

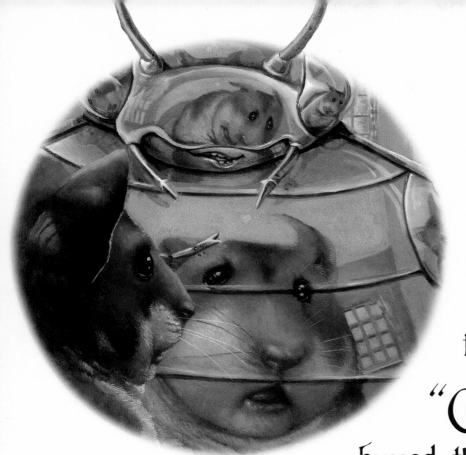

"I wish," said Scuttle, "that everything I touched turned to cheese."

"Cheese it is!" buzzed the beetle.

That night Scuttle forgot all about his silly wish.

But the next morning, Scuttle woke up to find his bed had turned to—

As soon as his feet
touched the floor,
it turned to

CHEESE!

Everything

he touched turned to . . .

CHEESE!

Was he dreaming?
Then he remembered the beetle.
Somehow his wish had really come true.
Scuttle started to touch
and eat everything in sight.

He ate and

ate and ate

and

ate.

And ate

and ate

and ate.

Soon Scuttle was very full.
And very thirsty.
He waddled up to Pounce's bowl for a drink.

But when his tongue touched the milk,
it turned to

CHEESE

"Uh-oh!" Scuttle squeaked.
"How will I ever drink again?"

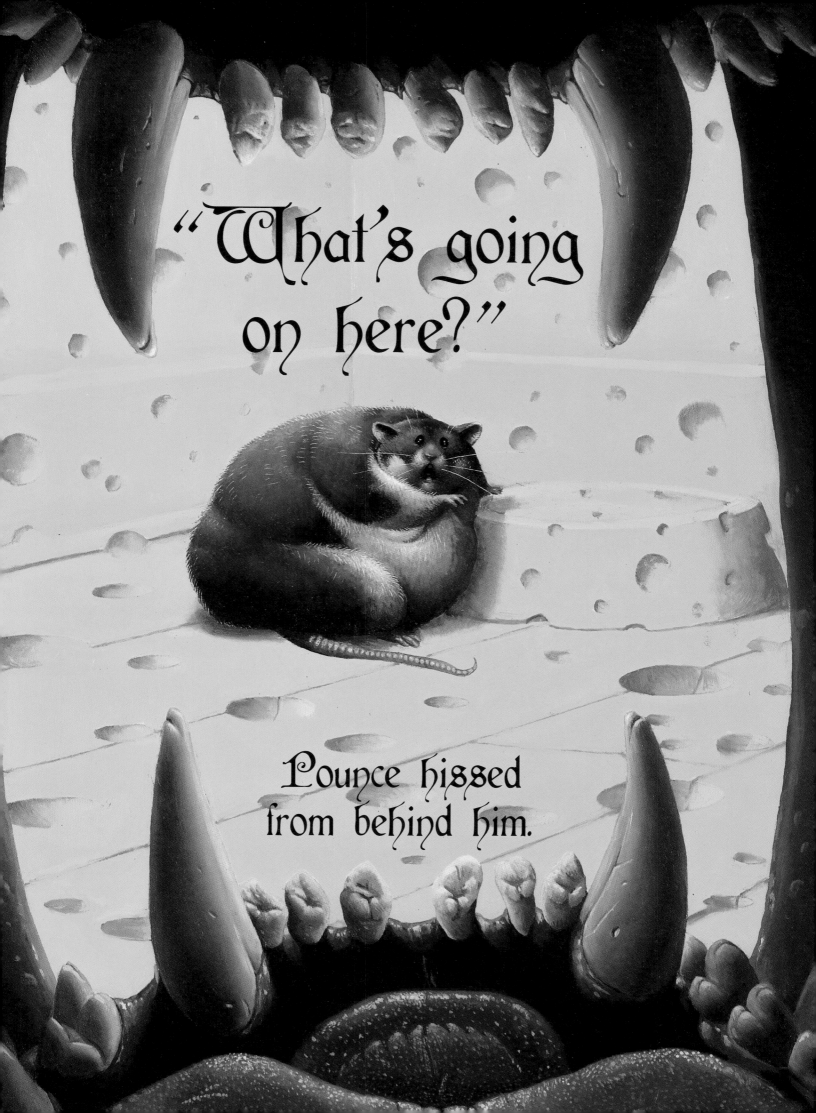

Scuttle turned to run,
but he couldn't
run fast anymore.

He couldn't run at all.

Pounce sniffed at him suspiciously.

He came closer and closer, until one of his whiskers brushed against Scuttle.

And then Pounce turned to—

CHEESE!

Tweet flew down to see what was wrong.

"No, Tweet! No!"
Scuttle squeaked.

"Stay away
from me!"

But it was too late.
And Tweet turned to—

Cheese.

Scuttle was miserable.

His wish had come true,
but it wasn't so
wonderful after all.
"What have I done?"
he cried.

"Take back my wish, Golden Beetle.
Oh, please, take it back!"

Scuttle heard a soft buzzing.
The beetle flew
into the room and . . .

suddenly
everything
changed back.

"Oh, Tweet,
you're back!
He did hear me,
after all!
Thank you,
Golden Beetle!"

Scuttle told Tweet the whole story. They both agreed that you have to be careful what you wish for. . .

For the
first time, Scuttle
realized how beautiful
the world was,
even if it's not
made of cheese.

He was very
happy that
everything
was back
to normal.

Well,
almost everything.

In loving memory of Scuttle,

who was tragically
devoured during the making
of this book.

ISBN-13: 978-0-545-00445-9
ISBN-10: 0-545-00445-4

Copyright © 2006 by Sean and Ryan Delonas.
All rights reserved. Published by Scholastic Inc., 557 Broadway, New York, NY 10012,
by arrangement with HarperCollins Publishers. SCHOLASTIC and associated logos
are trademarks and/or registered trademarks of Scholastic Inc.

12 11 10 9 8 7 6 5 4 3 2 1   7 8 9 10 11/0

Printed in the U.S.A.   08

First Scholastic printing, January 2007

Designed by P.R. Brown at Bau-Da Design Lab